PEPPER
THE PARROTFISH

A tale about a fish who changes the world by just being himself

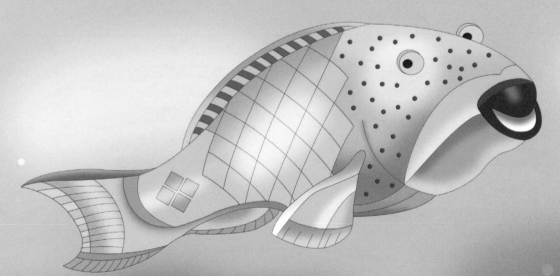

WRITTEN BY STEPHANIE ENSER
ILLUSTRATED BY MARK HOLLY

Published & distributed by:
Great Animal Trait LLC

in association with:
IBJ Book Publishing
41 E. Washington St., Suite 200
Indianapolis, IN 46204
www.ibjbp.com

Image used under license from
www.shutterstock.com.

Printed with environmentally friendly
vegetable-based ink.

ISBN 978-1-939550-74-3
First Edition

Library of Congress Control Number:
2017961069

Printed in the United States of America

Have you ever thought about the sand under your toes?
How did it get from the ocean to the beach and under your feet?

3

Follow that crab. She knows.
She knows about the sand
underneath your toes.

Carley the Crab scatters to the sandcastle contest.
She greets her friend Pepper The Parrotfish.

The tallest sandcastle wins.
The horn blows.
The contest begins.
Sandcastles are popping up everywhere!
Pepper and Carley need more sand to build
the tallest castle.

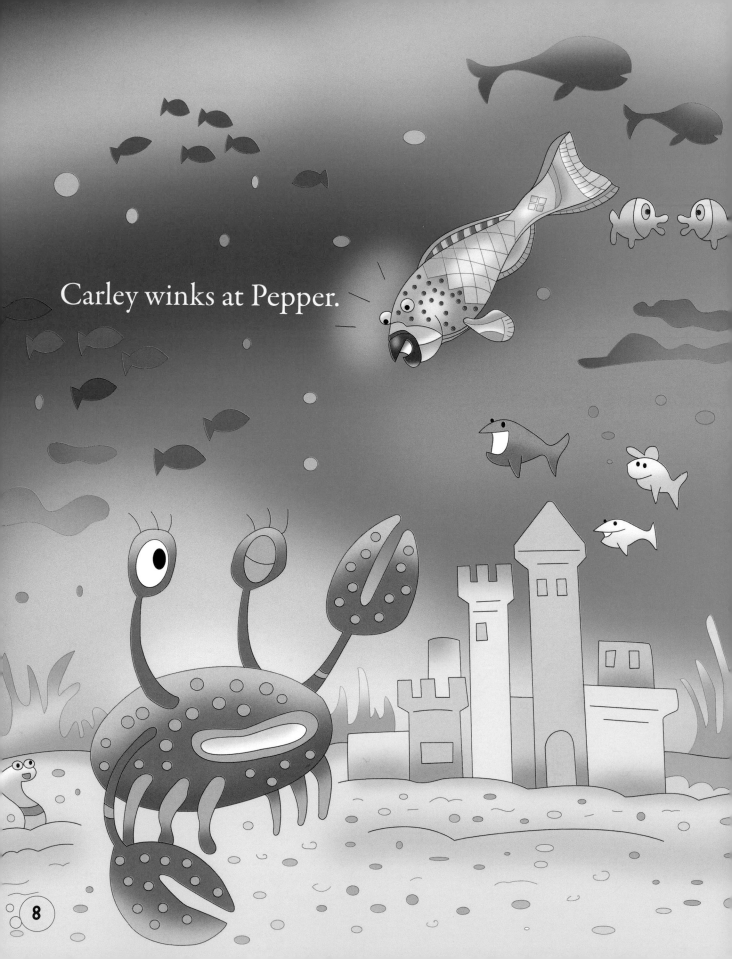

Carley winks at Pepper.

8

She knows what Pepper can do!
Pepper makes sand!

Pepper swims to the reef and
eats the algae, some coral too.

Crunch.
Crunch.
Crunch.
Swish.
Swish.
Swoosh.

The sand
falls down.

The
sandcastle
grows.

Do you think Pepper
made the sand that
was under your toes?

Pepper and Carley's sandcastle wins first place!
They proudly swim to Tully Turtle's birthday party.

Cake and ice cream fill their bellies while Tully opens presents.

Pepper wants to surprise Tully with a present.

Pepper swims to the coral reef.
Crunch.
Crunch.
Crunch.
Swish.
Swish.
Swoosh.

The sand falls fast.
Pepper is building sand dunes
taller than you can reach.

Do you think Pepper made the sand that was under your toes on the beach?

Tully snatches his sled and
Pepper jumps on back.

Sledding down the dunes is
Tully's favorite present!

21

What a fun day!
It is time for games
and popcorn.
A pajama party
before bed!

Sally Stingray forgot her sleeping bag. Pepper has an idea.

Pepper swims to the coral reef.
Crunch.
Crunch.
Crunch.
Swish.
Swish.
Swoosh.

The sand falls down.
Pepper is building
Sally a comfy bed
with a soft white
sheet.

Do you think Pepper made the sand that was under your feet?

Sally, Carley & Tully slumber cozy and warm.
Pepper dreams about making sand.

Pepper awakes and looks toward the beach.
He smiles at the people on the land.

Do you think they know
Pepper helps build their
beaches with sand?

Did you know that making sand
is something special Pepper can do?

Now, tell him
something special
that you can do too!

Pepper is a Parrotfish.
Pepper is special.
Pepper makes sand!

Pepper enjoys eating algae from our coral reefs.
He also eats part of the coral, which is easy to
do with his hard teeth.

He digests the nutrients and passes
the rest through his system.
Yes, he poos sand!
Although he is not the only animal
in the sea that makes sand, he
makes the most.

Clean Oceans...Healthy Coral...Happy Parrotfish...
BEAUTIFUL BEACHES!

Let's help the parrotfish make beautiful sandy beaches for all of us to enjoy by keeping our oceans clean and coral reefs healthy. A portion of the proceeds from the sale of this book will be donated towards marine conservation. Together we can make a difference!